Dear Paren

Congratulations! Your child is taking
the first steps on an exciting journey.
The destination? Independent reading!

STEP INTO READING® will help your child get there. The program offers
five steps to reading success. Each step includes fun stories and colorful
art or photographs. In addition to original fiction and books with favorite
characters, there are Step into Reading Non-Fiction Readers, Phonics Readers
and Boxed Sets, Sticker Readers, and Comic Readers—a complete literacy
program with something to interest every child.

Learning to Read, Step by Step!

Ready to Read   Preschool–Kindergarten
• big type and easy words • rhyme and rhythm • picture clues
For children who know the alphabet and are eager to
begin reading.

Reading with Help   Preschool–Grade 1
• basic vocabulary • short sentences • simple stories
For children who recognize familiar words and sound out
new words with help.

Reading on Your Own   Grades 1–3
• engaging characters • easy-to-follow plots • popular topics
For children who are ready to read on their own.

Reading Paragraphs   Grades 2–3
• challenging vocabulary • short paragraphs • exciting stories
For newly independent readers who read simple sentences
with confidence.

Ready for Chapters   Grades 2–4
• chapters • longer paragraphs • full-color art
For children who want to take the plunge into chapter books
but still like colorful pictures.

STEP INTO READING® is designed to give every child a successful
reading experience. The grade levels are only guides; children will progress
through the steps at their own speed, developing confidence in their reading.

Remember, a lifetime love of reading starts with a single step!

Special thanks to Ryan Ferguson, Debra Mostow Zakarin, Kristine Lombardi, Rita Lichtwardt, Nicole Corse, Karen Painter, Stuart Smith, Sammie Suchland, Charnita Belcher, Julia Phelps, Julia Pistor, Renata Marchand, Michelle Cogan, and Kris Fogel

Published in the United States by Random House Children's Books, a division of Penguin Random House LLC, 1745 Broadway, New York, NY 10019, and in Canada by Penguin Random House Canada Limited, Toronto.

Visit us on the Web!
StepIntoReading.com
randomhousekids.com

Educators and librarians, for a variety of teaching tools, visit us at RHTeachersLibrarians.com

ISBN 978-1-101-93995-6 (trade) — ISBN 978-1-101-93996-3 (lib. bdg.) — ISBN 978-1-101-93997-0 (ebook)

Printed in the United States of America
10 9 8 7 6 5 4 3 2 1

Barbie & HER SISTERS IN A PUPPY CHASE

Horses to the Rescue

Adapted by Devin Ann Wooster
Based on the screenplay by
Amy Wolfram and Kacey Arnold
Illustrated by Patrick Ian Moss
and The Artful Doodlers

Random House 🏠 New York

Chelsea flies to an island
for a dance contest.

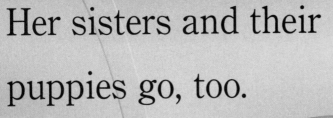

Her sisters and their puppies go, too.

There is a horse show
on the island.
Marco the trainer
rides Spirit.

Vivian trains Beauty.

Beauty dances.

The puppies dance, too!
They chase butterflies.

The puppies find an SUV.

It pulls the horse trailer.

The trainers drive away.

The puppies go, too!

The sisters must
find the lost puppies.
They follow the SUV.

Their cart gets stuck.

They have

to camp out.

The sisters camp
under the stars.
Barbie points
to the North Star.

The other stars move.

The North Star

always points north.

The next morning,
the girls hike
to find the puppies.
They zip down a cliff.

Chelsea is worried.

She wants to get

to the dance contest.

The girls
find the puppies!
The puppies
kiss the girls.

Chelsea is late
for her dance contest!
Vivian and Marco
will drive everyone.

Uh-oh!

The bridge is out.

The horses want
to help!
They can take the girls
to the dance contest.

The girls ride
the horses.
They are lost.
They cannot find
the dance stage.

The girls

see the North Star.

The dance stage is north.

They follow the star!

The girls reach
the dance contest.
Chelsea dances.
Her sisters dance, too.

The horses dance.

The puppies dance.

Everyone dances!

Thanks to her sisters
and her friends,
Chelsea wins the contest!